Prince Frederic

Jon Acevski and David Ashton

WARNER BOOKS

Prince Frederic
A Warner Book

First published in Great Britain in 1992 by Warner Books

Copyright © Hollywood Road Film Productions Limited 1992

The moral right of the authors has been asserted.

Design by Between The Lines
Illustrated by HRFP Artists

A CIP catalogue record for this book is available from the British Library.

ISBN 0 356 20114 7

Printed by Graphicom SRL, Italy

Warner Books
A Division of Little, Brown and Company (UK) Limited
165 Great Dover Street
London SE1 4YA

The Freddie Library

All Freddie books are available at your bookshop or newsagent, or can be ordered from:
Little, Brown and Company (UK) Limited, PO Box 11, Falmouth, Cornwall TR10 9EN.
Alternatively you may fax your order to the above address on: 0326 376423.

Payments can be made as follows: cheque, postal order (payable to Little, Brown and Company)
or credit card, Visa/Access, with card number and expiry date. Do not send cash or currency.
UK customers and BFPO allow £1.00 for postage and packing for the first book, plus 50p for the
second book, plus 30p for each additional book up to a maximum charge of £3.00 (7 books plus).
Overseas customers including Ireland, allow £2.00 for the first book
plus £1.00 for the second book plus 50p for each additional book.

Once upon a time in the country of France there lived a prince called Frederic.

His father, the great Magician King, was very sad at heart, for his queen had been drowned at sea the year before.

4

The boy was full of sorrow too, but he tried to cheer his father up with his magic tricks. Prince Frederic was almost as good a magician as the King.

Because of his special power he could sense that something evil was nearby . . . watching . . . waiting . . .

It was the King's sister, Messina. She also had the power of magic but hers, like the night, was black!

Prince Frederic had never forgotten that dreadful day when she had used her evil magic to turn the poor cat into a bird!

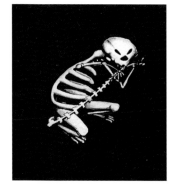
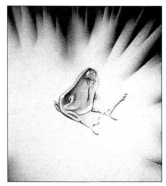

One morning, the King decided to take his son hunting.

Prince Frederic, riding his beautiful pony close behind his father, felt uneasy. The forest was so silent and strange.

Suddenly, from out of nowhere, a huge snake slithered in front of the King's horse. The frightened horse reared up and threw the King over the cliff, down to the rocks below.

Prince Frederic ran down the rocks to where his father lay. He had seen the snake and he knew that Messina was behind it all. But it was too late to save his poor father. The King was dead.

The whole kingdom mourned the great King. Noblemen from every corner of the land passed by to pay their respects as the King lay in state.

Prince Frederic tried not to cry but he could not hold back the tears. He ran to his father's coffin and sobbed. Then he felt Messina's hand on his shoulder and she led him away.

It was decided that Messina would rule the kingdom until Frederic was old enough to become King. But Messina had other plans . . . She locked all the doors to trap Frederic in his own castle.

Messina looked out of the window to make sure that it was too high for Frederic to jump down and escape. Then, looking in the mirror, she watched her wicked self change into a snake.

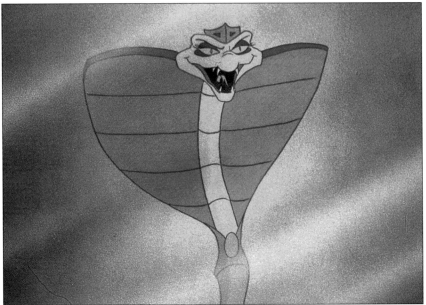

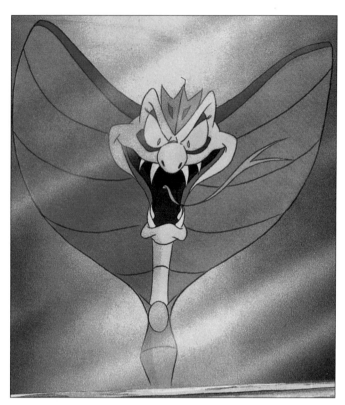

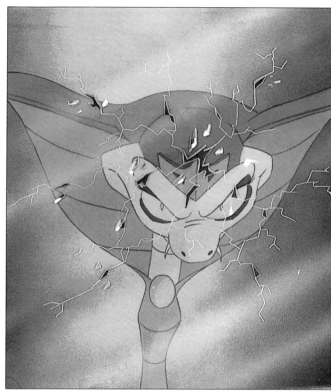

Suddenly the mirror shattered and the evil snake slithered towards Prince Frederic.

The Prince leapt back in terror as Messina's evil laughter echoed around the chamber.

The splinters of glass from the broken mirror flew to every corner of the room as though they were trying to escape from black-hearted Messina.

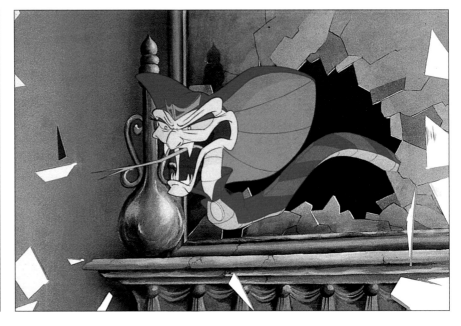

She fired a bolt of magic power at Frederic, but it missed him and he tried to hide. Messina changed back into her human form and, like a dark shadow, descended upon the terrified boy. With all her strength, she fired another bolt of magic lightning . . .

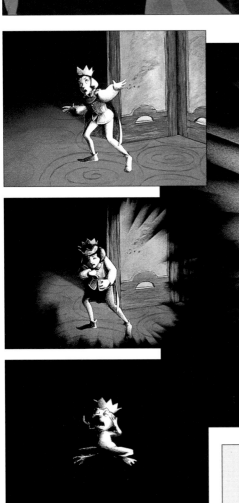

and Prince Frederic was no longer a boy prince but a frog prince. Messina laughed with delight. The helpless little frog did not know what to do.

Messina grabbed a plant pot and tried to trap the little frog inside to imprison him forever.

But Frederic managed to jump across the room out of the reach of his evil aunt.

He leapt a few times before he found the open window, for he was not used to being a frog.

As Messina ran after him in a fit of rage and hatred, Frederic looked down at the moat. He feared the water far below, but he was even more afraid of Messina, for he remembered what had happenend to his father.

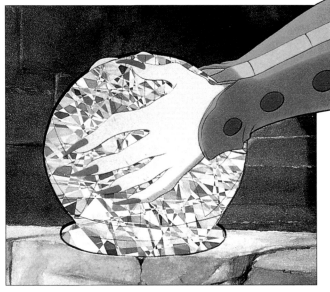

Messina slammed the pot down to trap the frog but it smashed into a thousand pieces. Frederic had no choice but to jump. Messina's rage was beyond control.

Down, down, down dropped Frederic towards the sea below. He held his nose as he disappeared under the murky water.

23

The furious Messina followed after Frederic. As she hit the water she changed back into a snake.

Messina was extremely angry with her nephew and chased after him. The little frog swam desperately through the water to avoid the horrible snake. Then he panicked and rushed up to the surface for air.

Frederic tried to swim away from the snake but he was not used to swimming as a frog and he kept bobbing up and down on the surface of the water. Messina lashed the sea into a violent storm and poor little Frederic was nearly crushed against the rocks.

Exhausted, Frederic hid behind one of the rocks as the furious snake slithered around, looking for him.

Suddenly Frederic heard his father's voice echoing in the distance.

"Swim, Frederic, fear not. Swim like a prince!"

Frederic thought he saw the image of his father in the movement of the underwater reeds.

The snake laughed and swam towards the King's shape, but it had vanished.

"That will not save him, brother dear!" hissed Messina.

Frederic looked and looked but he could not see his father again. He realised he was all alone and would have to fend for himself.

The sound of his father's voice had given him the strength he needed though. He swam on towards the open sea, but was closely followed by the evil snake.

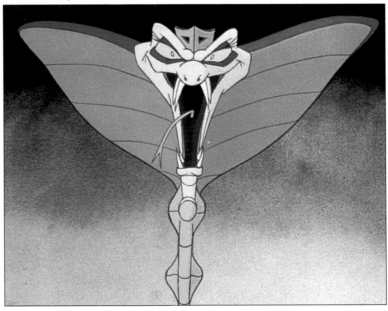

Frederic felt as if he had been swimming for hours and still that hateful snake was right behind him. He dived below and glanced around desperately and saw what looked like a black hole where he could hide.

He darted inside the hole. Hundreds of bubbles began to float towards him. Something strange was happening. The snake saw the bubbles too and swam closer. Frederic thought all was lost. Messina was going to catch him.

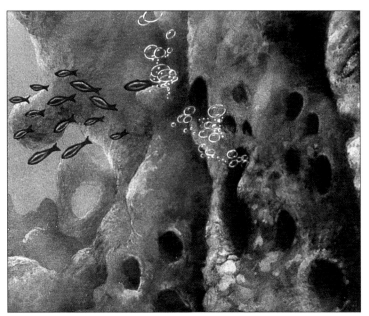

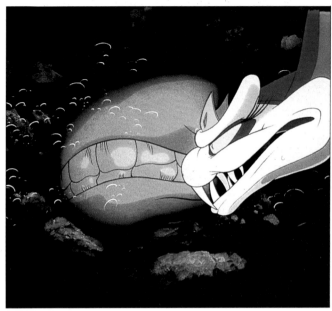

But as the snake reached into the hole, a huge set of teeth snapped together, almost chopping the snake's head off. The teeth belonged to a giant creature who rose from behind the rock. It was Nessie, the dinosaur from Loch Ness in Scotland.

The snake was furious. Her evil powers created a great whirling storm. Rocks began to swirl around, breaking from their foundations as though an earthquake had taken place.

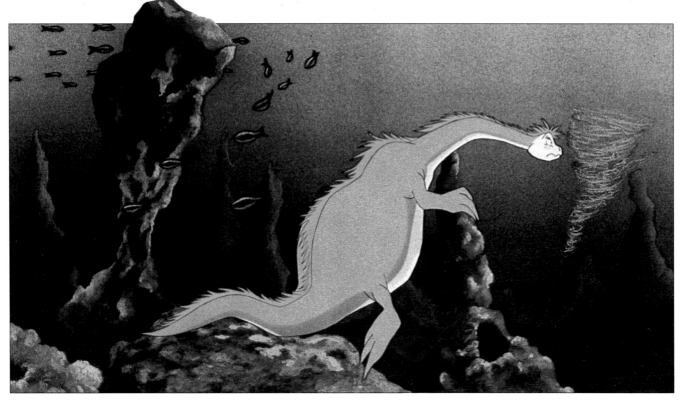

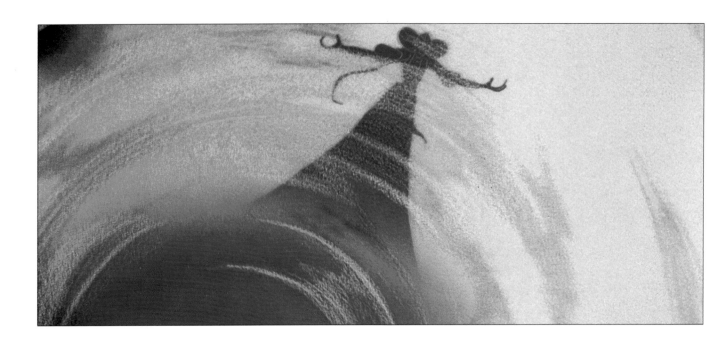

Then the snake changed back into Messina's human form and screamed, "You - little - ugly - frog! One day I will catch up with you and destroy you like I did your father and your mother, and then I shall be all-powerful. I shall rule the world!"

Then she fled back to the castle, the storm billowing around her, sinking a boat that happened to be in her path.

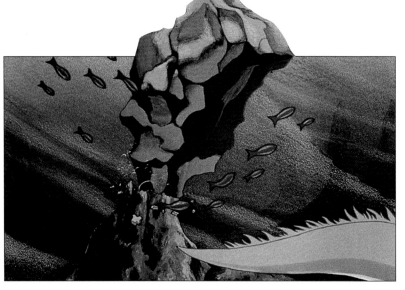

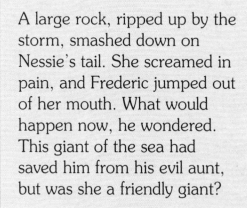

A large rock, ripped up by the storm, smashed down on Nessie's tail. She screamed in pain, and Frederic jumped out of her mouth. What would happen now, he wondered. This giant of the sea had saved him from his evil aunt, but was she a friendly giant?

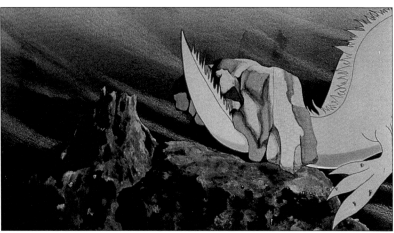

Frederic turned to the creature from the deep. The huge mouth was smiling now, and her gentle eyes calmed his fears.

"Hello, little frog," she said in a high sweet voice. "Don't be afraid, I won't hurt you." Frederic was suddenly carried away on a floating bubble, holding on for dear life.

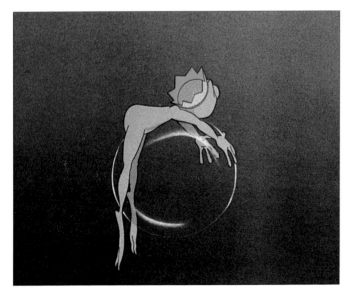

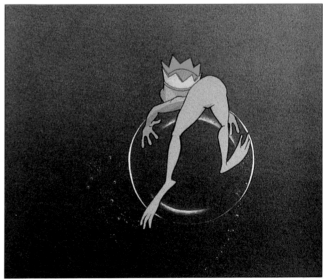

Nessie put out a flipper to stop him, and Frederic found that all his fear had gone.

"I'm not a frog, I'm a prince!" he explained proudly.

"Of course you are . . . of course you are. What's your name, little prince?" asked Nessie.

"Frederic - Frederic the Great!" he answered rather boastfully.

"Charmed, I'm sure, to meet you, Freddie," she said as she renamed the little frog. "My name's Nessie. How old are you?"

"Ten," said Freddie.

"That's funny, so am I."

They laughed together, a difference in size, but not in friendship.

"I have to go," said Freddie.

"Can I take you somewhere?" asked Nessie, but when she tried to move her long tail was still stuck firmly under the rock.

"Maybe I can help," offered Freddie.

Nessie laughed at the idea of the little frog being able to set her free, but he swam down towards her tail anyway. Freddie concentrated very, very, very hard . . .

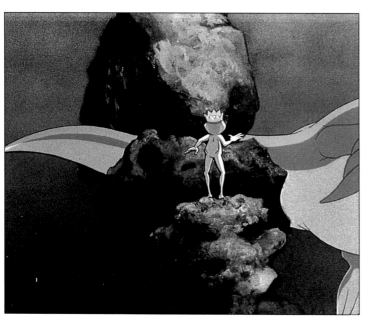

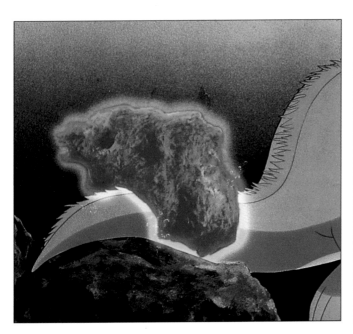
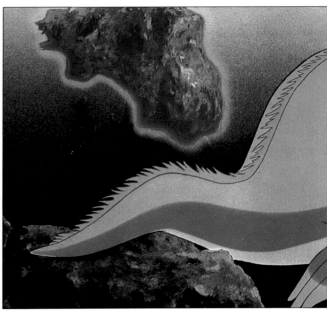

Slowly he raised the rock with his magical power. Nessie was amazed!

"This little frog is no ordinary frog," she thought as she pulled her tail from under the rock.

Freddie was exhausted, for using magic is a very tiring business. He collapsed on the rocks, but not for long.

The grateful Nessie lifted him gently in her flipper and headed for the surface. When Nessie's head was above water, Freddie hopped on top. He could see the stars twinkling in the dark sky.

"Well, this is as far as I can take you, Freddie. I have to get back home to bonnie Scotland, but if you ever need me, my dear, just whistle."
She whistled two notes and then she sang her name to the same tune.
"Ness-eee."

As the sound echoed against the sea waves, Nessie departed and Freddie was left alone to set out on his journey into the unknown.

Before long Freddie found his way to Frogland. When he arrived in the frog paradise, where music never ends, a frog orchestra was playing round a large pool, while frog dancers danced the Frog Rock. Freddie thought this would be a happy place to stay.

So Frederic
the Prince
began his
new life as
Freddie the
Frog.

Eager to make new friends, he jumped up on to the stage where two frogs danced and read the newspaper at the same time. Freddie thought it was a clever way of keeping up with the news.

Then Freddie hopped over to take a closer look at all the musicians in the orchestra. "Maybe one day I could do this," Freddie said to himself. "A drummer! That's what I would like to be when I grow up!"

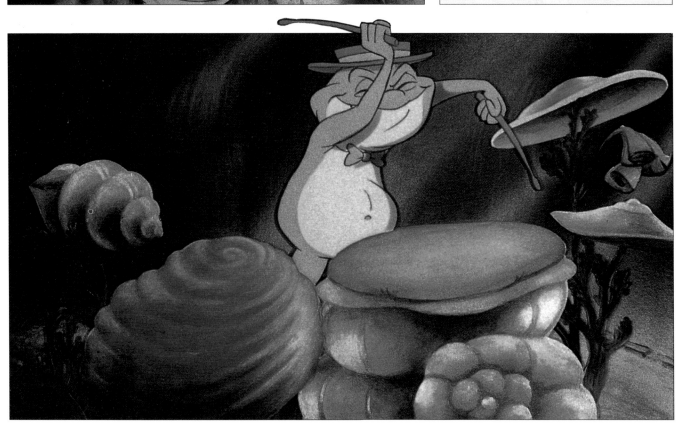

Freddie went on to a Frogland café. He thought he might also like to be a waiter. It looked so easy, leaping from lilypad to lilypad, serving drinks and balancing a tray at the same time.

"Too much waterlily wine," thought Freddie, as he watched a foolish amphibian trying to catch a fly.

Happy months passed, and winter came to Frogland. It was time for more fun.

"Let's build a snowfrog," a friend suggested. Freddie thought it was a very good idea.

But their snowy companion did not last long. A frog skier came hurtling down the slope, smack into the snowfrog.

"Oh, it hurts," sobbed the skier. Freddie thought it served him right for ruining their work of art.

Frogs are great skaters. They like any sport that has music, where you can twist and turn, leap and jump, dance and skip in the air.

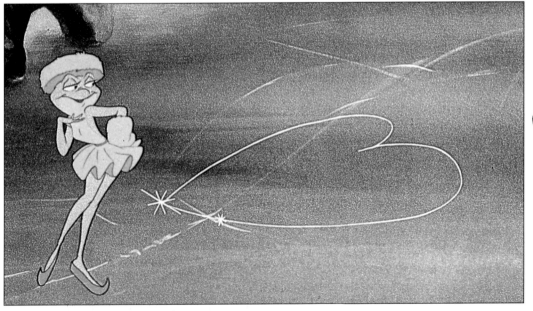

A lovely lady frog invited her friend to step into the heart she had skated on the ice. He did, but what a splash he made! However, a kiss made up for everything.

When all the snow had melted, spring was on its way - a time for joy and thrills in Frogland. In the pool the water was warm and it was great to slide down the rocks.

Somehow Freddie could not join in the game. He sat looking thoughtfully at the largest rock.

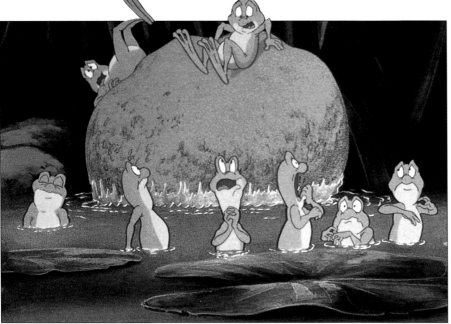

The rock began to glow and it rose up into the air.
    "Magic, magic!" shouted the chorus of frogs.

The huge rock floated obediently towards Freddie, then it began to crack, like a giant egg and exploded into millions of pieces!

The explosion had been silent - magical and dreamlike. The frogs were amazed.

"What power! What magic! What a frog you are, Freddie," they croaked admiringly. But Freddie had not carried out the trick to impress the other frogs. He wanted to see if his magic power still worked.

As time went on Freddie got used to being a frog, though sometimes he would remember his life as a prince. He knew he was different from the other frogs.

Frogland was still very special to Freddie -
he learned to share, he learned to laugh -
but he knew that one day he would have
to leave. Freddie was growing bigger.

He went on growing, and growing, and growing, to such a size that all the other frogs knew he was not a frog - not an ordinary one anyway.

The day he left, Freddie stood like a giant above the pond singing, "I am not a frog." All the frogs joined in the chorus, agreeing that Freddie was definitely not an ordinary frog!

Something had to be done about his clothes. In no time at all a shirt, a jacket, socks, shoes and a hat all appeared in front of Freddie. Frog tailors made sure that they were all designer clothes, of course.

The scarf! Where was the scarf? The scarf arrived in style, with a beautiful roll and swirl!

Freddie was transformed into a handsome man-frog. All his friends were sad to see him dressed in his new clothes because they knew he would be leaving them soon.

The magical Freddie was ready to set out on his adventures. His smile had a winning charm. His eyes had a vision of the future. He was ready to put his magic powers to good use.

So Freddie went into the
world, to fight evil,
wherever evil was to be
found.